The Life Cycle: A Journey's Tale

A Boy's Search for Midnight

Surprise! A Gift of Revenge

The Traveler: A Portal Fantasy

The Life Cycle: A Journey's Tale

The winter wind screams as it blows across my face. I open my eyes. Tears roll down my cheek and freeze. The cold travels along my spine. I shiver. A contagious echo of crying swells into my being. I cannot stop. Mother hums a soothing song. She warms my body and soul. I bellow a yawn and close my eyes.

I squint. It is another cold morning. Mother's vast arms do not protect me from the sun's rays. Talking and giggling ring through the winter's silence.

"Hello," I yell. The laughing stops. The wind whistles through Mother's branches.

"Go back to sleep, my children. It is not time to wake up." She begins to hum, and within a few minutes, we are asleep.

The warm rain splatters across my face as I take a long drink. My eyes are heavy. I am in a state of consciousness in between awake and asleep. I jolt awake from the sound of voices.

"Hello," I say.

"Welcome to the world of the living, sleepyhead," replies my Big Brother. The water droplets trickle along his many arms. He reminds me of a green star. I smile and then chuckle. My laugh starts soft, then it becomes louder and louder with each passing moment. My Brother stares at me.

"What's funny?" he asks.

"I don't know. A weird sensation to laugh is controlling my actions." He points to something below us.

"Do you see the orange-breasted creature?" I peer over the edge and then nod at him.

"Watch this." He spits an enormous loogie and it lands with a splat. The phlegm hangs from the creature's beak.

"Now that's funny," he says. We grin and spit a loogie together.

"Yip, yip," it says as the loogie bounces off its forehead and splatters into the left eye. We giggle as we sway in time with a cool breeze.

At the fork of Mother's great arms, the orange-breasted creature molds its home using small pieces of Mother it finds on the ground. It mixes dirt with spit to create a substance called mud to fill in any cracks. Whoa, it is a clever creature indeed.

The creature gathers green fluffy stuff from the ground to make a soft bed. It steals from Mother and the forest floor. It is evil and I do not trust it. What is it going to take next? One of my Brothers?

The bird stalks along the ground. With its keen eyes, it spots the slightest movement in the green fluffy stuff called grass. The bird plucks something from the dirt and swallows it. It is evil. It steals Mother's small arms and then takes her food. I do not know why, but I feel violated.

"Do not be so quick to judge, Little One." I pout and scowl at the bird. Where is the rain when you need it? Three turquoise-colored objects appear in the bird's home. They are not visible but they wink at me as it sits on them. Where did it steal the objects? The bird might be warming up its dessert. The objects must be strong or the bird is not heavy.

The squawking of three little mouths disturbs my sleep.

"Will you shut up?" I scream. Of course, they do not understand Mother's tongue. The Mother Bird returns with wiggling dirt creatures called worms and drops them into their open mouths. Ah, silence echoes through Mother's house. But how long will it last? Mother Bird has finally learned to give. She may not be evil, but we will see about the Little Rascals. They are loud and I can not sleep.

One of the Little Rascals gets reckless. He ventures out of his home and hops onto one of Mother's arms and snaps at one of my brothers until he has no arms left. The Little Rascal spits my brother out as if it is yesterday's trash. He peers at me. Uh, oh. What am I? Dessert? Do I look like a worm? He hops towards me and opens his beak as if he is going to take a bite.

"Mother, help." The Little Rascal clamps down on one of my arms. I become tense and try to resist. But it is of little use. My arm crumbles under his bite. He freezes. Mother Bird circles Mother before landing in the nest. The evil creature hops into the nest as my arm hangs on by a thread. He tries to act innocent.

One by one Mother Bird uses her beak to nudge the baby robins out of the nest. Good riddance. I hope they suffer an agonizing death. Revenge is a dish best... Six little wings flutter before my eyes.

"Yip, yip." My mouth drops open. I cannot believe it. The Little Rascals are flying. They circle Mother three times before soaring into the distance. I try to shake my fist at them. My arm floats to the ground.

The days become longer and hotter. The longer is not so bad, but the hotter is unbearable. I am not sure which is worse, the heat or the freezing temperatures. It has been several weeks since the Baby Birds left. It is possible that they do not remember their way home. I say good riddance. No sounds of new beast attacks on my brothers and sisters since the Baby Birds left. What can I really do?

A large furry bug is chomping on my brother. He differs from the robins. Chomps does not spit out my brother. Instead, he savors each bite as if it is his last. I feel the pain of my Brother as Chomps bites him again. The screams stop. The pain pauses.

He crawls to another victim and the screams begin again along with the pain. I have to sleep each night with the fear of waking up to a new missing brother or sister. He gets closer as each day passes. It might be better if Chomps swallows me now. I am exhausted from living each day with the anxiety that one-day Chomps will choose me for his meal.

Chomps crawls towards me. I do not think my heart can take this much longer. I may keel over and die long before he takes his first bite. Wow, he is fat. I need a needle so I can pop him like a balloon.

"Mother, Mother," I scream. Has she abandoned us? Are we pawns in a chess game? Chomps inches toward me with hungry eyes. Each step he takes brings me closer to my own death. He stops and wraps his feet around one of Mother's tiny arms. At first, he spins slowly and then he spins faster and faster until he becomes a blur. Chomps stops.

I go from hating him with a passion to… I am not sure what to think. The Crawling Garbage Disposal has a protective shell. He destroys everything in his path and then creates a fortress. The Little Rascals need to come back and peck at it. I glare at it with malice for a couple of weeks.

A whimpering sound echoes from inside. Something new emerges. Chomps is no longer a furry beastie. Instead, he has gone through a complete metamorphosis. He has vibrant colors dripping from his wet wings that he flaps back and forth.

I give the new creature the benefit of the doubt. If he does not harm any of my brothers or sisters, then he is alright in my book. I am still mesmerized by Chomps' beauty. The movements of his wings are hypnotic while my eyes follow the wings up and down, up and down… Lightning bugs blink on and off in unison to the crickets chirping. Where did Chomps go?

The days become cooler and shorter. I am covered with dew every morning. My body tingles as if I am going through a change. There is a buzz of excitement in the air and I cannot explain why. Perhaps it is the cooler temperatures.

Far below me are strange orange objects with happy and scary faces. Flashing lights and frightening noises do not allow me to sleep at night. My brothers and sisters are changing into something wonderful before my eyes. The green disappears and is replaced with vibrant colors of red, yellow, and orange. I smile and dance to the rhythm of the wind. My brothers and sisters join me. We are having a dance party.

The fiesta ends. Our colors fade and merge to create a solid light brown. Each day more and more brothers and sisters leave Mother and rest on the ground below. Our time with Mother has come to an end. A gentle breeze rocks me back and forth.

"Why must I leave you?"

"It's your time, Little One. Your Journey is almost complete." A burst of wind releases my grip and I float towards the ground. A gust blows me up, up, up towards Mother's great arms reaching to the sky. She looks at me and smiles.

"Go to sleep, Little One." I close my eyes one last time and drift to the hard ground to join my brothers and sisters.

My Journey is finally complete. And what a Journey it has been.

A Boy's Search for Midnight

"I am going to Todd's," I say.

"Stay away from the bank," my dad says.

"Yeah, yeah." I push the door along the trim so I do not break the glass. Last winter, he hit me with a horse crop for letting the door slam. The January cold blows in my face as I climb over the large snow pile that rests in front of the door. I prance across the street to Roy and Mary Stewart's house. Todd's grandmother answers the door and invites me into the kitchen.

"What are you baking?" I ask.

"Would you like some?"

"Do you even need to ask?" I reply with a smile. As I eat the cookies, Mary tells me about another memory of my mom. I heed to her every word, gesture, and pause so I can remember it later. It warms my heart to hear her talk about my mom in such a loving, caring manner.

I visit the Stewarts even when Todd is not visiting. It is my home away from home. They have been helping me with my aching heart. This might be the reason why I have not seen Todd in quite a while.

I scour for Midnight. She has been a loyal companion since my mom died. Me and Midnight play on the bank all the time. She is familiar with the area, but I am not. Midnight disappeared a week ago. My dad suspects she was killed by a car. I will not believe it until I see it with my own eyes.

Snow makes it difficult but not impossible to follow animal footprints. I wander through a maze of maple trees for about a hundred yards. A thin blanket of snow covers a stick at my feet. I hit a branch with it and the snow crumples at my feet. I tap my boots like Jim Rice and get into my best baseball stance and swing.

The snow tumbles on my head and It slides off my neck. The stick falls from my grip. A chill speeds along my spine. It is worse than a brain freeze from eating Rocky Road during the summer. I hate the winter with a passion.

Well... that's not completely true. I despise bees with a passion. During the winter, the stupid yellow jackets sleep. In school, they call it hibernating. Whatever name you use, it is sleeping.

One time when me and Todd went exploring, he stepped on a yellow jacket nest. The bees swarmed around my head. I ran home screaming and waving my arms. Those darn yellow jackets stung me 23 times and Todd did not even get stung once. He stood there laughing while I ran home waving my arms like a lunatic trying to escape from the nuthouse.

The next day, I punched him in the nose and refused to talk to him for a week.

"Midnight" I yell. I listen and wait. Nothing. Running water echoes from the bottom of the bank. I weave in and out of the maple trees. A set of fresh rabbit tracks lead me deeper and deeper into the tree line. I stop. Each bush and landmark looks the same.

What would Davy Crockett do? He is my favorite frontiersman. Todd likes Daniel Boone. It is too bad Davy

Crockett died at the Alamo. I grab a branch and shovel the snow. The thump of solid ground vibrates through my hands.

"What the hell, man." My homemade tool splits. I chip the dirt away from an exposed rock. My numb fingers pry the rock out of the dirt. It is not as sharp as I want, but it will have to do. Every so often, I scratch an arrow pointing up on a tree.

The Midday sun peers through the treetops. I squint. I walk into a tree and fall on my butt. A high pitch yelp followed by a low growl. That does not sound friendly. What did I blindside?

A St. Bernard hovers over me, baring its teeth. He drools as if I am lunch. His jaws inch closer and closer. I creep to my feet and sprint towards the edge of the bank. I'm going to die. I'm going to die.

The St. Bernard is on top of me. I land face first in the snow. I slip my arms out of my jacket and leap from the edge of the bank. Wow, that was close. The small branches from the ferns zoom by as I slide down the icy bank. It is as if I am looking down at the yellow lines while my dad drives the Starfire on Highway 91. If I do not slow down soon, I will not be able to stop.

My rubber boots are useless. I use my hands to angle myself towards a large root protruding at the base. I stop. Jaws shakes the jacket from side to side. Great, he has a new toy while I freeze to death. At least he has lost interest in me. He trots off, dragging his prize behind him.

####

Where is that boy? He has been gone too long. He has become too headstrong since his mother died. I still can't believe a police car killed her. I strut across the street and bang on the door.

"Good afternoon," Fr…

"My boy here?" I say.

"He left an …" I stomp away.

####

The stream winds like a snake upwards. A log covered with snow and ice lies across the brook. It has large branches which help me balance as I crossover. I have to use my arms like an airplane on my last few steps. I jump off the log and climb the opposite side of the bank.

The stream travels from Mascoma. If I follow the brook to the lake, I can find my way home. The climb is not as steep as the other side of the bank, but I have to test each step. The snow loads the maple branches. I grab the trunks to help me climb. The progress is slow and steady. A rock formation rises in the distance. It becomes larger and larger as I approach. This does not look promising.

The ice-covered rock formation blocks my path. There is no way I can climb it with my boots. I check my pockets for something to use, anything. I have come so far. There is no way I can go back the way I came. I pull out a nickel, a Jim Rice baseball card, and a RC bottle cap. Ooh, how much did I win? The RC is blank. Rats. I shuffle through my pockets one more time. They give me a present. It is a piece of metal with a Cub Scout emblem on the front. I forgot about you, my friend.

####

"Brendan, Brendan," I yell as I approach the bank at a brisk pace. That boy is going to be the death of me. He probably went searching for his dog. Those two are two peas in a pod. I told him to stay away from the bank. It's too dangerous.

The trail becomes familiar as Mascoma Lake comes into view. I grin to myself and quicken my pace. The path leads me up a short hill and then winds down to Mascoma. I pause. A faint whimpering echoes through the branches to my right. My head shakes while I walk closer. What am I doing? I have to hurry home for supper. The whining gets louder and louder with each step I take.

I get on my hands and knees and peer into a cage covered with branches. A dog shakes as she wags her tail. I slap my cheeks. My vision becomes hazy. I rest my head on her back and hug Midnight.

####

A St. Bernard trots along with a Boston Red Sox jacket drooping from his jaws.

"Brendan, Brendan," I yell in a panic. I run home as fast as a fat man can waddle.

"West Lebanon Police Department, what is your emergency?"

####

She is skinny and frail. How did Midnight survive in the cold without food? I would have died after the first day. The chills travel up my spine when Midnight's rough tongue kisses my cheeks. My hands shake while I scratch her behind the ears. I kiss her on the nose and urge her to follow me.

I am grateful she is alive, but my heart aches to watch her walk with a limp. The lake comes into view as we hobble around the bend. The trail leads us to the lake's edge. Midnight licks the ice. "Man, we are on the wrong side." We can either walk around or across the lake. I stare at Midnight for a moment.

I signal Midnight to walk with me across the ice. She sniffs it and then hobbles toward me. We hold our breath as we take our first step. Nothing happens. Then we take another step. Again, nothing happens. We exhale with relief. We continue our journey across the ice.

It is as if I can hear what Midnight is thinking. Are you sure this is a good idea? Something horrible is going to happen. I imagine the ice cracking and we fall through it. I peer at the shoreline while we trudge to the middle of the lake. We rest for a few minutes before moving forward.

The winter wind carries a sheet of snow across the ice. I shiver for a moment and then look at Midnight. I wish I still had my jacket. At least, I have a wool sweater. I like my cotton one better. It is not as itchy.

My muscles relax as we step onto solid ground and we continue to follow the path for thirty yards before it ends at a fork. Which way do we go? My dad always turns left. I call Midnight. She refuses to move. I walk towards her and she hobbles along the path leading to the right. "Are you sure?" I say. She peers back at me and trudges along. I quicken my step to catch up to her.

Oh, yeah, home. I am not too excited about facing my dad. By now, he knows I went down the bank. I'll bet my dad has a present waiting for me when I get home. He never acted like this when mom was alive. My dad is a different person. He makes me feel like he does not love me anymore.

"Hey, girl. Will you protect me from crazy Frank?" She looks at me and wags her tail. I smile and give her a good scratch behind her ears.

Traffic echoes through the trees as we step onto the pavement. We follow the highway to Main Street and then turn right on Seminary Hill. We quicken our pace. I cannot believe we made it. Spring Street is a distance of two laps around the bases. I blurt out random street names. We turn left on our street. My dad is talking with Roy Stewart in front of our house. I am in trouble.

A police car races towards us, flashing its lights and blaring its siren. I freeze. Midnight pushes me out of the way. The world around me slows d-o-w-n. I lose my balance and fall to the ground. Midnight flies through the air. I crawl over to Midnight and put her head in my lap. Her eyes are glassy and distant. My dad was right. She did get run over by a car, just like my mom. I stand up and walk away.

Surprise! A Gift of Revenge

I thumb through the mail. When am I going to get my Christmas bonus? I pause. A photograph of Stephen King's IT stares into my eyes. Creepy. Across the bottom, the word N-E-X-T is written in blood. Next? My fingers shake as I turn over the photo. It is blank. Who sent this? Is it a joke? Merry Christmas to me.

Rudolph the Red-Nosed Reindeer blares from Mr. Greene's garage stereo. He hammers the lights to the roof while balancing on the ladder. He waves and yells, "Merry Christmas." I wave and give him a short smile. He reminds me of a real-life Santa Clause.

The Jones boys maneuver a Christmas tree through the front door. Mrs. Jones directs them like a well-oiled machine. The twins hold hands and skip down the street. Nothing odd or weird. Wait a minute…

A man wearing a suit appears out of nowhere. He glares at me and smiles before driving away in his Mercedes. Creepy. Why does he look familiar? What is a lawyer type doing in my neighborhood?

####

What a b***h. The nerve of some people. How can she forget who I am after what she did to me. She doesn't recognize who... The cell phone chimes. I glance at the screen. F***k.

"Daddy are u sure you're gonna get me an ACS? Cuz the news said they're out of stock until March."

"No Worries Baby." Kersten needs the ACS. I have to get her one no matter what the consequences.

####

I whistle. Baby charges into the house and I scratch her behind the ears. She falls onto her back, exposing her belly. Her back leg jitters as I scratch her belly with my long nails.

I deadbolt the doors and test the burglar bars on the windows. What else can I do? Should I call the police?

Yeah, right. What evidence do I have? "Here officer, you can dust this photograph for fingerprints." Conspiracy Theory."

I hurry to the trash and grab a bottle of Coors Light and nudge it in between the handle and the deadbolt. I step back for a moment and inspect my handiwork. Awesome, I am desperate. What am I doing? I am mimicking a movie so I can keep myself safe. This has to be a prank. I remove the bottle from the door. There is no reason for me to be afraid. Then again, it never hurts to be safe. I put the bottle back.

####

I park in the fire lane of Pets-R-Us. A cheery teenager stands at the entrance bouncing a puppy in her arms. "Do you want to hold him," she asks. I brush past her. Why are there so many dog lovers in the world? Dogs are disgusting creatures. They sh** and shed everywhere. "You're a mean one, Mr. Grinch." plays over the store radio.

I rush down the different aisles. Looking. Searching. A hairy spider sits on a rock under a heat lamp. Tarantulas are intimidating, but can they kill? A few years ago, a tarantula moseyed into the garage while my ex-wife was cleaning it. She jumped on the table and yelled, "Frank." I grabbed the broom and swept it into our neighbor's yard. Those were better times.

The Reptile sign flashes. I blink and then smile slowly. You know me too well. I hurry down the aisle. The black mamba and king cobra cages are empty. F**k. Luck isn't on my side. I rush to the last cage and then pause. A boa lies underneath a heat lamp. I smirk as I flick my tongue like a snake.

####

My hands tremble as I guzzle a Coors Light and slam it on the kitchen counter. The foam spills over the neck and runs onto the linoleum. I pace back and forth between the Christmas tree and the kitchen. The photo stares back at me from the table. This is creepy. Why am I freaking out? It's only a picture, nothing more. Someone has to be playing a prank. The question is who?

I walk over to the tree and adjust the bow on my niece's present. Tiffany is going to love the Automated Computer System. She has been talking about it for months. It is like an Alexa but way better. How? I have no idea. All I know is that it's a fully functional computer-automated system. It might be Star Trek in a box.

Christmas Luck must have been on my side on Black Friday. I shoved my way through the crowds and snatched the last ACS in the city. Fox News reported that ACS will be out of stock until March. Some people might kill to get their hands on one. Is the photo related to the ACS? If so, how do they know I have one or where I live?

I tuck a kitchen knife under my pillow and pull the comforter over my head.

####

I sidestep the Christmas lights and hide in the shadows. It's a G** d*** football stadium. My crawling stops at the chain-link fence. A dog growls and bares its teeth. I throw a steak over the fence, back away, and return to my shadow and wait.

I peer through the backyard windows. Clever girl. Why does s*** have to be so G** d*** complicated? A chinaberry's limbs sprawl above the roof. I chuckle. "We have another way in my Pets."

I climb the tree with ease and drop onto the roof with a soft thud. The red brick winks at me through the layers of ash and soot. I unzip my backpack and lower it down the flue.

Snoring echoes across the yard. The St. Augustine crunches under my feet as I approach the dog sleeping against the house. My Buck knife reflects the blinking Christmas lights. "You're Next." I snicker.

####

I squint. A tarantula stares at me. My eyes widen. I flick the comforter. The hairy beast flies through the air. I sprint to the kitchen. "Die, you disgusting creature," I say as I swing my battle broom. The spider smashes against the wall and leaves a trail of guts.

I pull into the driveway. My feet and back ache. I toss the Walmart vest over the futon and heat a cup of green tea. I take a sip and relax on the futon. The Christmas ornaments echo the lights blinking in unison. Several of my decorations lie at the base of the tree. Interesting. They should not be falling already. It is a healthy tree. I stroll over to the tree and adjust an ornament. Two slits open.

I jump back and throw my hot tea into the Creature's eyes. It opens its jaws and hisses. I slam my teacup across the snake's mouth and it breaks in my hand. The boa coils around my legs. I hammer a cup fragment into its eye. It hisses and relaxes its grip. I run to the kitchen and clench my chopping knives.

I whistle for Baby from the back door. It is silent. "Baby," I yell. The wind whistles through the trees. Where is Baby? Did she get out somehow? "Baby, Baby," I yell as I ransack the backyard. Did I leave the gate open? Did she hop the fence? Surely Baby would never wander far. I stop. A blood river flows from the side of the house.

I sit on my knees. The echo of my heart racing rings in my ears. My hands shake as I wipe the tears that bubble to the surface. "Oh, Baby, oh Baby," I cry over and over. I fall on my ribs and curl into a ball.

My vision is blurry. A small swarm of flies buzz around my face. I swat them away. Blood is everywhere but where is Baby? A blood trail saturates the grass. It leads to the fence and then stops. How is that even possible? A black android vibrates.

I stare at the screen for a moment. "Hello?" I say. It is silent. Background noise echoes through the speaker.

"Hello?" I say again. The phone disconnects. The last couple of days have been terrifying. This is more than a prank. Who is trying to kill me? I scroll through the missed calls. Kersten called 15 times. Who is she? I dial the number.

"Daddy I've been calling you all day. Where are you?" I swipe the disconnect. Who's phone is this? Are you the man in the Mercedes? Why do you look familiar? I tap my forehead. Think, Alex, think.

Of, course. Black Friday. I snatched the last ACS from this guy. He was about to grab it when I swiped it.

"Hey, I was about to grab that you b***. he yelled. I smiled and ran to the checkout counter at the front of the store. He must have followed me home. I stomp back and forth. I halt inches from the boa.

It lies dead on the carpet, oozing from the gashes along its neck and abdomen. I kick it. Mr. Greene goes deer hunting. He might like some fresh snake. Yum, yum, in the tum. I drag the boa into the backyard and kick it a few more times.

####

I race across Braes Bayou. Where is my phone? My coat pocket is empty. Sh***. Where is it? I dig in all my pockets and shuffle papers around in the glove compartment. No phone. It must have fallen out at the b***'s house.

I zoom along South Post Oak and turn left into my parents' neighborhood. A red brick house sits on the corner. The tires squeal as I pull into the garage. I pop the trunk. The Christmas present is in the way. I set the box in the passenger seat, grab the Hefty bag and sling it over my shoulder.

I cross the street and follow the path in between several houses for about twenty yards. To my left, are three houses sitting on the neighborhood's old playground. We used to play baseball in the summer and football in the fall. Those were the rules and everyone followed them.

I whistle a familiar tune as I cross the street one more time and mosey along the old trail for about ten minutes before it ends at the bayou's edge. Rotten eggs resonate from the water. I hold my breath and heave the bag into the current... The current carries it downstream.

I speed along the freeway and pat a box sitting in the passenger seat. The b***** is going to love my present. Merry f****** Christmas to me. "I wish you a Merry Christmas. I wish you..."

####

I scroll through the Facebook page on the phone and then pause. Gotcha. I have a face to go with a name. That's weird. Frank, what are you hiding? I snap a screenshot.

The doorbell rings. I am not expecting anyone. My heart can not stand any more trauma today. I turn on the outside lights and scan the entry through the peephole. No one is there. I open the door a few inches. A Christmas package rests on the porch.

A present for me. Frank, you shouldn't have. I carry it into the house and place it in the center of the living room. I pace around the box. The rapid echo of my heartbeat rings in my ears. Beads of sweat drip into my eyes. I stop pacing. What surprise does he have in store for me? Only one way to find out. Baby gazes back at me. I grab my android. I don't remember dialing. The phone rings.

"Houston Police Department, what is your emergency?" I ramble about the boa and Baby. "Someone is trying to kill me." He transfers me.

"Detective Jim Jeffries, how can I help you?" I begin again.

"Frank is trying to kill me. I do not know his last name." He stops me.

"Do you have a recent photo?"

"Yes, I do."

"Text it to me at 713****.

I text him the picture. He stops talking. I wait. It seems like an eternity. All I can hear is his breathing.

"Are you still there?" No answer. This is a waste of time. My finger hovers over the disconnect button.

"I'm coming over."

"Huh?"

"What's your address?"

I pace between the front door and the living room. I scan the front yard. The detective needs to hurry. What if Frank appears? He is sadistic. The beer bottle splatters to the floor.

"Little b*****, little b*****, let me in." I sprint to the kitchen and snatch two knives from the cutting block.

"I'm ready for ya. You crazy son of a..."

Frank crashes through the door. He strolls through the doorway with a sinister grin. Really. A battering ram. I turn and run out the back door. I trip over the boa.

Frank's firm hands push me into the ground. I struggle from his grip but it is no use. Frank flips me over and snarls. He places a knife against my throat.

"You are going die b**."

"Frank, where are you?"

"Over here, Jim." A middle-aged man in a khaki suit walks over to me and smiles. "Nice to meet you, Alex. I would shake your hand, but you seem to be on edge."

Frank and Jim chuckle.

The Traveler: A Portal Fantasy

I sit on my Huffy Stingray staring at the 45-degree hill. I'm going to kill myself. This went so much better in my head. Besides, I have taken all the precautions. I have my football helmet, my Evel Knievel pajamas, and my emerald amulet that my grams gave me before she died. She told me it would protect me. I do not believe it is true. But it never hurts to be safe.

I exhale and lift my feet off the ground. My tires echo against the asphalt. The mountain road winds and dips like the Texas Cyclone. The houses zip by in a blur of black and white. MY handlebars shake from side to side. I tighten my grip as the downtown traffic echoes through the stretch of the last 50 yards.

The cars drive back and forth as I brake. The chain falls off. My muscles become tense. I ride through the blinking red light and close my eyes. Everything becomes as dark as night.

####

The thunder awakens the night sky. Lightning flashes through the cabin's doorway. I clutch my chest and roll onto the dirt floor into a ball. It feels like a giant hand is squeezing and twisting my heart. The pain is unbearable.

My legs shake as I crawl to my feet and I stumble out of the cabin. The thunder vibrates under me. The suffering intensifies. I collapse.

####

The ocean is pitch black. My eyes burn, but I keep them open. A faint light below me is a distance of about 30 yards. With a swift kick, I dive. A school of strange-looking fish swims past me. My chest feels like it is going to explode. I cannot hold my breath much longer. My arms and legs throb with pain. I gasp.

The midafternoon sun shines… wait a minute. The moon is where the sun should be. It's bright and radiates heat. What kind of place is this?

My grams said the amulet would protect me. She forgot to mention that I would be transported to another world. I have had enough adventure to last a lifetime. All I wanted to do was pretend I was Evel Knievel and ride down Seminary Hill. If the amulet brought me here, it can send me home.

I squeeze my eyes and think of my bedroom. Nothing. I try again. This time, I grip the amulet. Nothing. I peer at it. "How are we going to get home?" First things first. I need to find dry land.

Birds fly overhead and dive intermittently. Smoke rises on the horizon. I swim using a lackadaisical backstroke. My dad taught me how to use my hands and legs in a relaxed manner. He said that I could swim for hours using his version of the backstroke. I stop and turn around. The shoreline is about 200 yards away.

####

The stench of dung fills my nostrils. I spring to my feet. Great, I collapsed in a pile of poo. Several wolves lie across the meadow. What the fairies is going on?

I creep up to one of the wolves. "Hey," I yell. It doesn't move. Maybe a sound sleeper. I kick it. Nope, it's not sleeping. What the fairies. Who killed them? How is that even possible? They're fierce fighters...

I kneel next to one of the wolves. A blanket of black ash covers the pack. It's as someone roasted them over a fire. Fairy magic. I jog across the meadow to my cabin.

####

A stick jabs me in my shoulder. I turn over. It pokes me in the butt.

"What the hell." I open my eyes.

"You dead?" says an old fox wearing a tunic. Where in tarnation am I? Talking foxes?

I sit up and he says, "Are you elfish? Show me your ears." I squint and glare at him. He hits me over the head with his cane.

"Now, boy." I hesitate before pulling a clump of silver hair away from my left ear. He glares for an instant and hobbles up the beach. I gawk at him in disbelief. What in tarnation is an elf? He stops and glances back at me.

"You com'n?"

####

I sit at the table and gaze at my black fingertips. What the fairies. My magic never creates this kind of reaction. Besides, I haven't used it in quite some time. Steam rises from the hot water cooking on the fire. I rise from my stump and pour the boiling water into a mug filled with fairy herbs. They fizzle as they mix with the hot water.

I pinch my nose as I guzzle the herb tea.

A boy with silver hair crawls out of the ocean. He's a mirror image of myself except for the foreign garments he wears. Red pokes him with his cane. Doppelganger.

It makes sense. The pain from the night before, the charred wolves, and my fingertips turning black. The Doppelganger must be from another world. He's going to kill us all.

####

The fox taps the ground in front of the fire and says, "sit."

He hobbles over to a dusty trunk and drops dry clothes in my lap. The old fox shuffles over to a pot and dishes out a pot of fish stew. "Thanks." He nods and limps to the table.

My stomach rumbles. I devour the food and change out of my pajamas.

"What were you do'in in the sea?" he says.

"Swimming."

"Swimm'n? The sea is fer fish'n."

"What is your name?" I say.

"Red." I snicker.

"What's yours?" he says in an angry tone.

"asa."

"asa? You're no Asa."

Red stands and hobbles out the doorway. Who is this other asa? I saunter to the door and peer at the beach. Hundreds of charred fish lie along the shore. That is not normal. Something weird is going on. Red stands at the water and pokes a fish with his cane.

He enters the hut and growls, "Where are you from, boy?" I pause. Here we go again. I thought we were through with this.

"The other side of the ocean," I whisper.

"What? Speak up, boy."

"The other side of the ocean," I say a little louder.

"What the elves." Red hobbles over to where I am standing and cracks me over the head with his cane. He stares at my amulet. Red flicks the amulet with his cane.

"Where did you get this?"

I shrug and say, "I have no idea"

"Don't be smart wit me."

"My Grams."

"Does she have pointy ears and silver hair?" he says with an icy tone.

"Huh? No."

"You may not be elfin but you used its evil magic. Creatures are dy'n cuz of you." Red snarls.

"What are you talking about?"

"The amulet."

"What about it?"

"Don't talk back. I know bout its power."

"I already tried. It does not work." He glares at me for a moment and then pokes at the

fire with a stick.

"We've gotta see the Emerald Dragon. He'll know what to do."

"Dragon? Where is this dragon?"

"Emerald Mountains." I snicker. "You think this is funny?" He swings his cane at me. I catch it. He pulls out a sword. I whack him over the head with his cane. He stumbles. I grab the stew from the fire and throw it at him. Red screams. The sword slips from his grip as he falls. I clench the sword and lay the point at his throat.

"You may not be elfin but you have the speed of an elf." I strike him on the head with the blunt end of the sword.

####

I don my traveling cloak and fill my pockets with healing herbs. Around my neck, I drop three elf stones into a pouch. I sheath a dirk in each boot and rush out the doorway.

#####

With the scabbard in my hand, I run away from Red's hut. My head races with my thoughts. I have to climb the mountains and find the Emerald Dragon. I stop and peer at the horizon. Green-blue minerals dance in the moonlight. At least, I know which direction to go.

####

I tromp up the beach and into Red's hut. He lies sprawled on the floor, covered in the stew. I kick him with my boot. He grunts and stares at me.

"Asa?"

"Looks like my doppelganger got the best of you." I grimace.

"He's an elf. He's too quick ta be anything else."

"Where did he go?"

"Dunno. He knocked me out wit me own sword."

"You're lying, Red." I smile and rub my fingers together. Smoke manifests within the hut.

"Ok, ok. No dream magic. He went search'n fer the dragon."

I grin and slap him on the cheek. "Thanks, Red."

The Emerald Dragon. This is serious. My doppelganger thinks it will solve his problem. He does not need to consult the dragon. The solution is simple. I have to kill him. Two people can not exist in the same realm at the same time. Why can't he figure this out for himself? There is only one true Asa, and that's me.

####

I weave in and out of the pine and maple trees. The charred leaves crumble beneath my feet. I need to hurry. Red might try to… wait a minute. An old fox with a cane attempting to run. That is more comical than a reality. What did he say? I'm killing creatures. He must have meant the fish. What else could he mean? Did I kill other animals as well?

The river echoes through the forest. Water droplets fill my nostrils. The trees create a doorway I must pass through.

The current ripples in the opposite direction than I expected. It does not flow into the ocean. Instead, it flows upward toward the Emerald Mountains.

A plank of wood winks at me. I drag a weathered raft onto the riverbed. It can not be this easy. I ride up the mountain, have a friendly chat with the dragon, and then it sends me home. I lie down and close my eyes.

How fast is elf speed and how did I get it? My dad has auburn hair and egg-shaped ears. Grams had silver hair, but old people have silver hair. And her ears were not pointed. It is possible that she had elf ears at one time. Grams did have scars on the top of both of her ears. Whenever I asked her about it, she always avoided the subject. Wholly Mackerel. I am an elf. How come I can not do magic? I thought all elves have some kind of power.

The moon sleeps behind the mountains. The sun rises and comes out to play with the stars. A male lion's roar echoes across the river. I lie flat on the raft and hope it does not see me. An alligator with tusks and a fishtail swims next to me. I hold my breath and squeeze my eyes shut.

####

I track my doppelganger to the river. He left obvious signs on the ground and on the trees. It's almost like he is inviting me to follow him and kill him. It's too easy. I may not have to do it. Emerald Island will do it for me.

The river is like my illusion magic. My Doppelganger will feel safe riding up the mountain. Then, wham! He goes over the waterfall and is eaten by the creatures of Emerald Island.

The allusks are an interesting breed. They dislike their food to move or squirm. They will roll my doppelganger over and over and then stuff him under a rock or log to gnaw on later.

The lions enjoy hunting in prides. They will tear him apart piece by piece. It's very likely that they'll start eating him before he's dead.

My gut says that he'll survive. After all, he's my doppelganger. He's smart, resilient, and incredibly handsome. The more likely reason is that he'll discover illusion magic. I'm going to wait for him where he feels safe.

####

The morning moonlight shines in my eyes. I squint and place my arm over them. The water moves faster. I sit up with a start. Two allusks swim in the opposite direction. Interesting. The river rumbles in the distance. What is that? I balance on the raft and shield my eyes from the moon. Nothing to see but the ripples of the water churning and foaming as it crashes against the rocks. Something bad is going to happen. I can feel it.

My fingers grip the edge of the raft while I lie on my stomach. I turn forward and backward as I ride the current. It is a real-life water park. The front of the raft lifts and crashes. The water sprays in my face and the river s-l-o-w-s down.

Everything around me is moving in slow motion. I scream. The water's momentum carries me over the waterfall. I squeeze my eyes shut and wait to fall into the water. It is like jumping off a high dive at my dad's work but it takes longer to crash through the water. I am still falling and my fingers clench the raft. Right before the raft crashes, I dive.

The force of the water forces me down. I open my eyes. A green glow winks at me. I swim towards it. I break through the water with a gasp. Green gems and minerals illuminate the cavern's wall. Emerald stalactites hang from the ceiling.

The vibration of the rumbling waterfall fills the cavern. I swim along the surface for about 200 hundred yards. The tavern ends. A wall blocks me from traveling any further. I have come so far. There must be another way. I must hug my dad.

The wall. is as smooth as glass. I follow it to an open space along the bottom and squeeze through. A lion standing at the watering hole stumbles at the sight of me. I smile and bark like a dog. He turns and runs in the opposite direction. That was not a good idea. The lions will return in greater numbers. I scamper out of the pool. Large maple trees surround the pool and hide it from plain view. I have stumbled upon the pride's secret. They will kill me to protect it. Things are getting more complicated.

A roar echoes behind me. Six male lions surround me. Instead of walking on all fours, they stand upright like a man. Each of them carries a battle-ax. They hiss and snarl as they toss their axes from paw to paw.

My first reaction is to back away. Instead, I giggle. I know I am supposed to be scared. The lions are not intimidating. It does not mean I will not die. They remind me of *Thunder, Thunder, Thundercats*. They roar and attack with their battle-axes raised.

"Freeze," I say.

They stop. I tiptoe in between the frozen lions. What in tarnation? Did I do this? "Spin." The lions spin like ballerinas. "Lie down." The lions lie down. I smile and clap my hands. This is going to be good.

"Bring me food." The smell of grilled meat fills the air. My stomach growls. A lioness sets a plate in front of me. I face the pride and say, "You do not remember me. Go to the falls and take a nap." The pride turns and strolls away.

I travel a short distance before I leave the forest at my heels. The hills roll like waves in the ocean leading to the Emerald Mountain. I climb the first slope with ease. The next incline is a little more difficult. The air is no longer warm. It is not cold either. I pause and decide to slip off my shoes and let the grass inch its way in between my toes.

A shadow casts over the valley. The moon should be shining. The sun and the moon are getting ready to kiss. Strange. A herd of white horses grazes in the valley. A black stallion stands watch. I walk clear of the herd. Hoofbeats echo behind me. I turn around and the stallion stops inches away from my nose.

It is not a stallion. A greenhorn protrudes from its forehead.

"Does it hurt?" I reach over to touch it. The unicorn backs away.

"You can see my horn?" it says.

"Can't everyone?"

"You must have powerful magic. Only the truly gifted can lay eyes on it."

"You are the most beautiful creature I have ever seen." I attempt to hug the black unicorn. He steps back a few steps.

"Do you think I am a horse?" He escorts me to the base of the Emerald Mountain. I give him a quick hug and he does not back away. Instead, he gives a reassuring smile as I turn to run along the trail. The path winds like a coil of rope. Why was the unicorn nice to me?

The sun and moon are almost one. They cast a dark shadow over the valley. Something different is in the air. A tingling sensation travels throughout my fingers.

I climb the stone path. A weathered fence winds up the mountain. If I fall, an old piece of rope is going to keep me from smashing my brains in. Wow, what a sturdy railing. As the trail becomes more difficult to climb, I grab hold of the steel steaks in the center of the path. Each step I take brings me closer to my goal.

The trail ends at an opening illuminated by an emerald glow. I advance into the cave. A snake-boy appears at the entrance. He flicks his tongue and hisses. I step back for a moment.

"Freeze," I say. He disappears in a puff of gray smoke and a mirror image of myself emerges. I hesitate for a second or two.

"You must be the infamous Doppelganger," he says.

"What? I did not hear you. I'm asa. What do you want?"

"It is simple. You are going to die." I lose my footing for a moment.

"What? Why?" Asa chuckles.

"You are my doppelganger. My world is dying because of you." He grabs a dirk from his boot and smirks. I sprint past him into the cave. He scampers at my heels. A sharp pain attacks my hamstring and I stumble to the ground. He yanks the dirk out of my leg and pushes the knife against my throat.

I snatch two green rocks and box his ears. The dirk slips from his fingers and he falls on his side. I push my knee on his throat and stab his leg. "Ahh," he groans.

"How do you like it?"

"Enough," says the Emerald Dragon. His nostrils flare inches from my face and his eyes change from a yellow to a red. He glares at each of us. I inch myself to my feet.

"You two will kill each other."

"That's the plan," says Asa. The Emerald Dragon peers at him. Asa's wounds drip on the cave floor. I look at him and smirk. The Emerald Dragon gawks at me.

"What do you desire?"

"I want to go home," I say.

"Use your amulet."

"I tried in the ocean. It does not work." The Emerald Dragon chuckles.

"Of course it didn't work. Magic needs time to recharge. Didn't you sense the magic during the eclipse?"

I grab my amulet and think of my room. The cave fades. I'm going... Asa jerks it out of my hands and laughs. He holds the amulet and disappears in a puff of smoke.

Reader, thank you for taking the time to read my book. if you enjoyed it, please leave a review.

If you would like to be part of my email list, please contact me at reubenshupp@yahoo.com or twitter.com/rshupp50.